I0624410

NOT FADE AWAY

HELL or HIGH WATER: BOOK 3.5

SE JAKES

RIPTIDE
PUBLISHING

Riptide Publishing
PO Box 6652
Hillsborough, NJ 08844
www.riptidepublishing.com

Not Fade Away (Hell or High Water, #3.5)

Cover Art by L.C. Chase, lcchase.com/design.htm
Editor: Sarah Frantz
Layout: L.C. Chase, lcchase.com/design.htm

ISBN: 978-1-62649-220-2

First edition
August, 2014

Also available in ebook:
ISBN: 978-1-62649-099-4

CHAPTER ONE

The truth is rarely pure and never simple.
—Oscar Wilde

Prophet rolled off Tommy and onto the mattress, pretty sure he was a broken man . . . for the next hour or two, at least. "Jesus Christ, you're trying to kill me with sex."

Tom groaned. "Your fault. You're the one who brought up that damned game of Truth or Dare." He held up his white T-shirt and waved it around in an *I surrender* motion.

"That's not going to help." Prophet tried to rise. "And as soon as I can move again, I'll prove it." He collapsed with his cheek against the mattress. "Where are the sheets?"

Tom turned and tucked his head against Prophet's shoulder. "Did we fuck the sheets off the bed? How is that possible?"

"Voodoo," Prophet mumbled. "Blame it on the voodoo." He carded a heavy hand through Tommy's hair and felt his cock actually stir like it was some kind of motherfucking superhero. "And that fucking game . . ."

Months earlier . . .

Tom had been back from New Orleans and that hurricane—and Dave and Roger's eyeballing—for three weeks. With Prophet. At Prophet's apartment, since he'd been unceremoniously evicted from his own place. Prophet had helped move his boxes. Had even forced him to unpack them, for the first time in forever. And it'd all been surprisingly easy.

And *easy* and *Prophet* were words Tom would never typically put into the same sentence.

Ever.

But that night started easy as well, with a bottle of Jack Daniel's Green Label between them, and Prophet setting shots on fire. Tom didn't remember how or why that started, but there was an ice storm brewing outside. An early one for the season.

And then Prophet'd suggested an innocent game of Truth or Dare.

"I'm not playing Truth or Dare with you," Tom told him seriously. "Not while we're stuck here—"

"Wait a second—now being with me is 'being stuck'?" Prophet pointed the bottle at Tom. "I'll have you know there are plenty of people who wouldn't mind 'being stuck' here with me."

Tom crossed his arms. "Besides me, name them."

Prophet narrowed his eyes. "You say that like it'll be hard."

"You're deflecting. And procrastinating."

Prophet's smile was all cat with canary feathers sticking out of its mouth. "Cillian."

Tom stood. "You'll pay for that, Elijah Henry Drews."

"Wrong." Prophet's voice was laced with satisfaction. "Keep guessing, but you'll never know my middle name. I'll never even tell you if I have one or not." He leaned forward, his elbows on the table, his voice low and huskier now. "But you're so fucking easy, Tommy. Truth or dare."

"No way—you first. Truth or dare. Choose, or I'll choose for you."

Prophet rolled his eyes. "Fine. Truth."

It was Tom's turn to smile. "Tell me about the favors."

"What favors?"

"You know exactly what I'm talking about. The favors you do for Mal when you owe him."

"Oh, those favors." Prophet smirked. "You really want to know, Tommy?"

"Wouldn't ask if I didn't."

"First . . . truth or dare."

Tom gave one of his best weight-of-the-world sighs that he'd learned from Prophet. "That's not how the game works."

"It's how it works with me. My rules." Prophet poured another shot and threatened to light it on fire. "Truth or dare, or this flaming shot?"

It was Tom's turn to roll his eyes. "Guess which I'll pick."

"Dare, of course."

"Exactly."

"Good. Perfect. Thanks for being predictable."

Tom gave him a smirk, especially because he could hear the anticipation in Prophet's voice no matter how much Prophet tried to hide it. "Fuck you and your predictable."

"Yes, *fucking* will play into it, I'm sure." Prophet raked his gaze up and down Tom's body, with that fucking look he got in his eyes that told Tom he was in for a long, long night. "I think we can both get what we want."

"I'm waiting."

"Your dare—go steal Cillian's couch back and bring it up here."

"You're not serious."

Prophet shrugged and tried a look that was obviously supposed to be innocent—a look that'd never quite worked, even before Tom knew him as well as he did. "Hey, you mentioned it."

"I never mentioned Cillian—or his stupid couch," Tom corrected, then realized it was pointless to argue. "Fine. Not a problem." Prophet sat back and motioned toward the door. "Why do I have to do my dare before I get your truth?"

"Because you didn't want to play this game in the first place."

"First of all, that makes no sense. Second of all, you're such a fucking pain in my ass. Swear to Christ." Tom stalked out of the house and down the stairs to Cillian's place. "Turn the fucking alarm off, yeah?"

"Whatever!" Prophet called back.

Tom waited a beat, said a silent prayer that Prophet had done as he asked, and then used the extra key he'd snagged on the way down to open Cillian's door. It was heavy steel and slid just like Prophet's. And thankfully the couch sat front and center as if it was waiting for this moment, under a light of its own like some kind of insane trophy, right in the middle of the living room.

He pushed it out of the room easily enough—there might've been a lamp casualty, but he gave it the finger and kept moving. Wrestling the couch to the stairs wasn't that hard, but carrying it up would be a bitch. He got behind it and tried a combination push / slide, but no, the way the back was structured didn't make for a smooth ride.

Still, it was the best way, beyond strapping the fucking thing to his back, which he seriously considered. He was cursing enough to make Prophet laugh, and by that point, Tom was so pissed off he didn't care about Prophet's truth—or anyone's goddamned truth—at all. He only cared about taking Prophet on this fucking couch and making sure that if Cillian was monitoring the situation, he'd see something to blow his mind.

He lifted the end and then pushed as hard as he could, the couch bouncing up each stair with a hard slam. When it got stuck, he put his entire weight against it sharp and fast, like he was a human battering ram, before realizing that the arm was half-caught against the bannister and yeah, there went the arm.

Fuck it. Didn't need that arm anyway. He pushed and shoved and got the couch into Prophet's apartment, leaving it in the middle of the foyer before turning to grab the arm from the landing. He came inside again to slide the apartment door shut before semi reattaching the arm by pushing it back onto the exposed nails.

Prophet was watching, grinning unabashedly. Until Tom went and switched on the alarm . . . and the cameras. And then stripped his shirt off and said, "You. Couch. Now."

Huh, no more laughing. Shocking. Just Prophet's intense gaze as Tom gave out more directions. "And take your clothes off before you get here."

"Giving orders?"

"You don't like that?"

Prophet rolled his eyes. "It's like you don't know me at all."

"Your cock likes it, though." Tom waited, hands on his hips. "Seems to know *me* quite well."

Prophet's cock was also a complete traitor . . . and a slut for the tattooed, pierced, handsome-as-fuck Cajun-drawling man in front of him.

Tom was breathing hard, but it honestly didn't look like half carrying the goddamned couch up the stairs had caused him any strain.

Granted, it never had to Prophet either, but he hired movers to do it each time. Pay someone enough, and they didn't ask questions.

Then again, the movers didn't take their shirts off the way Tom was doing now . . . or look like Tom.

Tom unbuttoned his jeans, unzipped them a bit and left them hanging open enough for Prophet to note the lack of underwear. "Nice," he managed. "You can keep going."

"You first, Prophet."

Fine. Two could—and would—play at this game. Prophet took his shirt off, flinging it to the floor with a flourish, and then unbuttoned his jeans. Left them the way Tom had his. Because he could tease just as well. Better, even.

But Tom's next words held more than an edge of warning. "I'll throw you over my shoulder and bring you here if I have to." Even though they were only maybe twenty-feet apart, Tom would do it too. And Prophet might want to let him.

But hell, he wasn't going to let Tommy know that, so he walked toward him like he was bored of the entire thing. Even though he could—and most likely would—come if Tommy touched him.

Tom waited until he was right in front of him, then said, "No fucking way, Proph—you're not coming until I say you are."

"How the hell . . .?" Right. Cajun voodoo crap.

Tom smiled, then reached down and unzipped Prophet's jeans the rest of the way. Then he pushed them off Prophet's hips while Prophet willed himself not to come.

"Step out of them," Tom ordered, and Prophet did, kicking them to the side.

Tom appraised him in a most appreciative way that Prophet swore made his entire body blush.

"Turn around, Proph—hands on the cushions."

Prophet swallowed. Okay, nearly swallowed his own tongue too, but managed, "Even if Cillian *was* watching, you know he turned the camera off on his end the second you told me to strip."

Tom growled, low in his throat. "Yeah. And that was two seconds too long."

"You're going to make this couch suffer, aren't you?"

Tommy smiled. "Definitely."

"But me first."

"Yeah, Proph, you're always first."

Prophet stared at him for a beat longer, unmoving, before Tom's hand snaked around his wrist, a firm grip but not a painful one. He looked at Tom and swallowed hard at the unabashed, naked heat in his eyes.

And then he let Tom guide him to face the back of the couch. Tom's palm pressed down between his shoulder blades. He conceded slightly by leaning forward to hold fast to the couch's back, but he didn't bend over the couch, the way he knew Tom wanted him to. Because Tom was not the boss of him.

Not all the time.

And not now. This was his game, dammit.

Behind him, Tom snorted softly. "Still fighting compliance?"

"I *am* complying." He somehow managed to sound halfway agreeable, albeit through clenched teeth. He felt Tom's hands slide down his sides and land on his hips before his legs were kicked apart. And then Tom must've gotten on his knees behind him because he was holding Prophet's ass cheeks apart, sliding his tongue inside . . . "Fuck."

Tom gripped him tightly as he tongued him, his fingers digging into Prophet's skin as the rimming intensified, both sensations sparking nerve endings. Prophet fought like hell to keep his legs from trembling as Tom speared his tongue to work him harder. And then Tom pulled back, causing Prophet to groan.

Tom chuckled softly, then pressed a thumb inside him, which made Prophet go up on his toes. Tom tugged him back down by a hip. And then he worked his other thumb inside, and Prophet stilled completely.

Tom slid his thumbs in and out of him, pressing, then stretching, and Prophet flushed with embarrassment and pleasure all at once at the exploration.

Finally, Tom took his thumbs out, then licked him again before burying his face in Prophet's ass and holy motherfucking hell. His cock was leaking, begging for him to touch it, but somehow he knew Tom wouldn't want that.

And somehow, he complied with Tom's rules. As Tom worked him, Prophet couldn't help that his upper body slid lower, so his fists were touching the seat cushions. He made sure his cock wasn't touching the back of the couch, because any friction would send him over the edge.

True to form, Tom reached around to torture him, playing with his cockhead, running a finger around the crown.

"Gonna come if you do that," Prophet told him, his voice husky to his own ears.

"Not allowed to," Tom reminded him.

"Then don't fucking touch me."

"You're not making these rules, *bébé*." Tom's tongue dragged up his spine, too lightly to be anything but squirm-inducing. And then he began to bite the taut skin along Prophet's back, biting, sucking, claiming...

It was the same area he'd been drawing on, almost obsessively. Definitely mapping out his space on Prophet's body.

"Marking me?" Prophet asked, like he did every time. Because he liked to hear Tom's answer.

"Better fucking believe it. Problem?"

"Fuck. No. No problem."

"Good." Tom's finger slid inside of him. At some point, he'd lubed his fingers, so a second finger quickly joined it. Tom twisted them as he worked them back and forth, with Prophet rocking gently to his easy rhythm.

"Tommy, please..."

Tom kicked his legs open more, forcing him to go palms down on the cushions of this motherfucking, no-good-for-anything-or-anyone couch, and he heard the rip of a condom wrapper. Seconds later, Tom pushed the thick head of his cock inside him. Prophet went on his toes, trying to gain any kind of purchase as Tom's cock filled him. The couch was in front of him, Tom behind him ... and the rest was a tenuous balance.

And Tommy had him. So fucking strong. One of the few men Prophet knew—or could admit—was just as strong as he was.

Or maybe stronger. He could feel the strength in Tom's hold. Knew he'd have bruises. He'd feel this for days, all the reminder he needed that he was cared for. *Well* cared for.

He'd give Tom the same reminder, because Prophet wasn't the only one who needed it.

Tom was precariously close to coming himself and fuck no, he didn't want this to end. Not yet.

Instead, he pulled out and grabbed Prophet around the chest, forcing him to straighten up. He bit the side of his neck, sucked hard. And then he took Prophet's hand, forced him to fist it, leaving his pointer finger out. Then he took Prophet's wrist and made him circle his finger around his own leaking cock, catching pre-cum. Then he tugged Prophet's hand up to his mouth and said, "Open."

Prophet did. Guiding him, he watched Prophet rub his finger along his own tongue. And then Tom moved Prophet's hand out of the way, turned Prophet's head to the side so he could put his own mouth on Prophet's, licking the man's tongue.

Prophet groaned and bucked his ass back against him. Tom knew it was killing him not to come. "Good, Proph. So fucking good watching you like this . . . all easy for me."

"You're so dirty, T."

"For you."

"You so fucking love this."

"And you push me to it on goddamned purpose," Tom ground out.

Prophet shrugged his answer.

Tom kissed him fiercely. Because he didn't really need Proph to answer anyway. Prophet didn't have to ask for what he wanted, because he knew Tom would know how—and when—to give it to him. And that kind of trust? Tom wouldn't have it any other way.

Finally, he broke the kiss, patted Prophet's ass, noting his legs were trembling. "Come on. Couch. On your hands and knees, *bébé*." Prophet half turned his face so Tom could see the clench in his jaw. "You started this, Proph. I'm just trying to finish it. Unless you don't want to finish . . ."

His voice must've held the right amount of lust and warning, because Prophet grunted, then grudgingly walked around to the front of the couch and carefully climbed on, the barely reattached arm groaning against his weight.

On his hands and knees, head bowed, Prophet managed to look vulnerable and in control at the same time, the muscles on his back bunching under his tanned shoulders. Tom's fingers itched to draw again as much as his cock wanted to come. The eternal fight between sex and art, he supposed. Which is why he'd always liked combining them.

He satisfied himself momentarily by tracing the now-familiar patterns on Prophet's skin after climbing onto the cushions behind him. The dreamcatcher he envisioned under the right shoulder blade that would run along his side to feather on his ribs . . .

"I don't understand why you're trying to motherfucking kill me," Prophet growled. And it was an unmistakable show of temper. And it turned Tom the fuck on, more than he'd already been.

Tom wound an arm around him, jerked Prophet hard against him, rubbing his cock against Prophet's ass, prepared to fuck him until Prophet screamed his name.

"Smile for the camera." He yanked Prophet's hair, not needing to see Prophet's face to know exactly what he looked like in this moment.

Cillian wasn't seeing any of this, but owning Prophet this way was too good of a dare to resist.

He put his hand between Prophet's shoulder blades, pressing him down to his elbows—they were sliding forward anyway, since the arm on the couch wasn't holding well under their combined weight—and the angle allowed him to sink into Prophet, so hot and tight. Soon, nothing would come between them. For now, he'd pretend there wasn't a condom there.

Because Prophet came to New Orleans for him. In turn, Prophet needed to be shown exactly how Tom felt . . . and Tom would do so, as often as necessary. He also wouldn't forget that this all started with a game. "Let's talk about your favors."

"Talk? You're . . . fucking . . . kidding me."

"I did my dare. Isn't it time for your truth?" God, it was getting harder to think—he slowed his thrusts, which made Prophet groan with frustration and punch the arm of the couch in front of him.

Which made it partially come off, and Tom had to grab his hips hard to keep from sliding out of him.

"Tommy, come on." Prophet dug in, pushing his hips back against Tom, a testament to Prophet's strength since Tom was pretty much holding him immobile. "Fuck that truth for tonight. This . . . this is truth to me right now."

Tom stilled, wondering how Prophet could just floor him in an instant. He reached around to palm Prophet's cock. Tugged a few times. "And this is my truth for now, but it's not where this ends."

Prophet laughed, then groaned. "Is that how it's gonna be?"

"I'll tell you exactly how it's gonna be," Tom drawled as Prophet's body stiffened under him, then shuddered uncontrollably as Tom held him tight. "Yeah, let go . . . got you."

"I know you do, Tommy."

Tom knew that was the only reason Prophet could actually let go at all . . . and it made Tom at once honored and more fiercely protective of this man than ever.

CHAPTER TWO

Present day

Tom looked around the wreckage of the room. "Fuck, you know this always happens when you mention that game, Proph."

"At least you didn't light the couch on fire again and almost burn the place to the ground." Prophet's tone was close to a reprimand.

Tom stared at him. "Seriously? I threw it out the window immediately—into the ice storm—so I still don't see the reason for your freak-out, princess." Prophet raised his brows, but Tom continued, "And that burn down the middle of the kitchen table? That didn't almost set us on fire?"

"I put it out," Prophet said calmly. "And stop talking about it. You're making me want to fuck you again, and I'll die if I do that. And it'll be on your head."

"Don't talk about heads if you don't want to have sex," Tom shot back. Because yes, the mere mention of that night always had them reliving it.

That Truth or Dare night had ended in more sex. Because yeah, the combination of bed and Prophet was *never* a bad way to end anything. Even if it was a bed, like now, completely stripped of any coverings, sheets, pillows . . . It looked like . . . Holy hell, the room looked like a hurricane hit it.

Or a tornado. His own goddamned personal one. And even though that made him smile, something else caught in his memory, and he raised his head and snapped his fingers. "Wait a minute."

Prophet opened his eyes. "You know what happened to the sheets?"

"No. I never got my truth that night."

"I got your truth right here." Prophet rolled onto his side and pointed between his legs.

"You're twelve. I swear."

"There are no twelve year olds packing this, T."

"Not even you when you were twelve?"

Prophet smiled smugly. "I was an exception."

"Yes, you're definitely the exception. And don't try to change the subject. You owe me a truth."

"The statute of limitations on that game expired."

"Really, Mr. Exception?"

Prophet smiled. "I like that name. You can keep calling me that."

"Truth. Where is mine?"

"It was a game."

"I carried a motherfucking couch on my back."

"Really? Now we're lying about couch-carrying abilities?" Prophet shook his head sadly. "I'm so disappointed. We all know you pushed it up the stairs. And really, what did it ever do to you but bring you pleasure."

Tom stared at him, the way he imagined he would a mental patient. Which really wasn't that far off from what he was dealing with. "Now I get two truths."

"How do you figure that?"

"It's like interest."

Prophet sighed, turned away, and began rooting around as he hung over the side of the bed. "Where are the pillows? How can you fuck away pillows? That's inhuman. Unholy."

"Right. So two truths. I want to know what the favors you do for Mal entail. And I want to know the last time you did one for him."

Prophet shifted, still rooting around on the floor for the sheets and pillows, his ass almost in Tom's face, which at any other time might be appealing . . . until, "I take him to BDSM clubs. And two weeks ago."

Tom was reaching out to grab Prophet's ass. At Proph's words, he pulled back, thought about it, and slapped it. Hard. Prophet howled and turned, and Tom narrowed his eyes, feeling more than a little irritated. And yes, pissed at himself for bringing it all up in the first place. "Really? Two weeks ago?"

"Yeah, really. He asked."

"Didn't realize you owed him so much."

"I'll always owe him. Jesus, aren't you two getting along now?"

"That's not the point." Tom pushed off the bed and Prophet rolled onto his back.

"See? You ruined a perfectly good night with the motherfucking truth!"

"We are never playing—or talking—about that game again. Ever!" Tom called over his shoulder as he walked out of the room.

"And he calls me a princess." Prophet sighed as he stared up at the ceiling, listening to Tommy stomp around in the living room. He got off the bed and stepped over a tangle of what were once the bedcovers to grab a pair of shorts from his dresser.

He pulled them on once he got into the kitchen, where Tom stood, still naked and drinking straight from the OJ container. Typically that bothered Tom more than Prophet, who figured that hey, they shared enough bodily fluids that this kind of thing shouldn't matter.

"What's your problem?" he asked as Tom continued to ignore him, even after he put the juice back in the fridge.

That got Tom to finally ground out, "Really? You're coming at me with attitude?"

"Yes," Prophet said evenly.

Tom tilted his head and pointed at Prophet. "So let me get this straight. We're supposed to be watching out for danger at every turn. Not going anywhere without backup. Not supposed to leave ourselves vulnerable."

"Your point?"

"And you're out doing *favors* with Mal."

"Right. So he's not vulnerable."

"How the fuck do you make this sound so rational?"

"Because it is." Prophet heard the edge in his tone but it wouldn't matter—Tom wasn't going to let it go that easily. No, he'd find a way to overanalyze something that was, really and truly, goddamned simple.

"Are you fucking kidding me?"

And there it was. "No."

Tom threw his hands in the air. "You told me about the favors. It's implied that they're sexual. And I'm just supposed to walk away and let that shit happen? Fuck that. Fuck you."

"Tom—" He followed Tom into the living room, where he'd been marching away.

Tom turned to him . . . and on him. "No. Is that why Mal and I are so much alike to you?"

"You've got things in common, but you're not alike to me at all. Not like that." Prophet clenched his jaw after he spoke.

"Don't ask me to trust you. That's bullshit."

Prophet's voice softened when he said, "That's not . . . Mal and I don't *do* anything together. I'm just there for him, to make sure nothing happens while he . . . Fuck, he doesn't always know his limits, okay? It's not about sex at all." He paused, realized he was confusing shit needlessly, then broke it down to the basic, "I'm not cheating, T."

Tom knew that. Understood it on every rational level he had, but irrational Tom rose up, stronger, burning hotter, and decided that he should be completely, irrationally pissed. And jealous. And if Mal were around? Tom definitely would've used his hands to talk.

As long as they were going for truth . . . "All those times you've done this before, did you go out and fuck someone's brains out after?"

Prophet stared at him. "Yeah, I did." And then, "But this last one? It's the first time I've done this for Mal since you and I met."

They'd never talked about exclusivity. It'd just happened. And while he didn't feel betrayed by what Prophet had *done*, his stomach was in knots because Proph hadn't *told* him.

Then again, it wasn't only Prophet's secret to tell.

Fuck.

Prophet gave a small shrug and walked away into the bedroom. If Tom wanted to fight more, he'd have to follow.

But if he was done fighting, at least for tonight?

He shifted, leaned against the couch. Thought about sleeping out here tonight, but he'd learned too much about wasted time to let that happen. Instead, he went and got into the bed . . . and wrapped around Prophet, who looked surprised. "Hey. No bad dreams tonight."

Surprised, with a small smile. "You think?"

Did he? He'd asked for a truth, gotten it . . . and then gotten pissed, which was always, he knew, Prophet's biggest fear of the truth. So Tom's anger had been directed at the wrong person—at least some of it—and hell, he didn't need to fuck with any more of Prophet's sleep. "I'll make sure of it," he said fiercely, and he'd never meant anything more in his life.

CHAPTER THREE

T om wasn't just mad. No, the bastard was planning on getting even. Prophet could sense the fuck out of that shit.

Two days later, he was waiting on Tom to get home from the EE offices when Tom called him instead.

Sounding, if not a little drunk, then definitely loose. "Hey, Proph. What's up?"

"You called me, Tom. Where are you?"

"Club."

"Club?" Prophet echoed suspiciously.

"Place you took Mal, I think."

What the fuck? "Jesus, T." Tommy and a BDSM club was trouble. The kind that made his dick hard.

"Come meet me for a drink," Tom demanded belligerently.

Pissed and a little drunk. Not a good combo. "Get in a cab and come home."

"Nope. You'll have to come for a drink."

Fuck me. "Fine. Make it a shot. And then I'm dragging you home."

"And putting me over your knee?" Tommy's deep, slightly drunk drawl jolted Prophet. How had Tommy wrapped him so thoroughly around his finger?

"I'm coming."

"Yeah, you are."

"Tommy, Christ." He hung up, grabbed the keys to his truck, and then stared down at them. Sighed. Put them back in the drawer and called a cab.

Because his eyes would betray him. Over and over, and each time it would be a surprise. But he couldn't worry about that now, because there was plenty of other shit in the way.

He was carrying, because he had concealed weapons permits, enough of them to wallpaper his apartment. There hadn't been any activity though, not since they'd discovered that John was, in fact, alive and well and occasionally visiting Prophet's room, among other places.

So his nerves were set on high before he walked in. When he opened the door, scanned the room, he quickly spotted what was his. Flirting heavily at the bar. And obviously waiting and watching for Prophet, since he waved happily to him.

Seemed like Tom's hurt and anger over last night's admissions had faded away somewhat easily.

Too easily. And Prophet wasn't fooled, but he was pissed that Tom would try to fool him to get him pissed.

Because really, Tom was *here*, the place that was literally the whole source of the fight. And even though it was more of a symbol of a bigger issue, it was still fucking weird being here with Tom, because this wasn't a place he associated with Tom. He wouldn't do this with Tom—not in a club, anyway, and not even in a private room. And Tom wouldn't want it here, either. Having Tom here was . . . Prophet didn't know how to explain it. Because Tom and Mal needed a lot of the same things, but they weren't the *same*. No way.

"Hey baby. Looking for a daddy?" Prophet looked up at a big man wearing full leathers. A definite bear. Handsome too. "Saw you here a couple of weeks ago. I'm Ray."

"Yeah?" Prophet had two options here, and the one that'd piss Tom off the most won. "Why don't you buy me a drink, Ray?"

He was a quick three shots in when a hand clasped on the back of his neck. Normally, the urge to grab it, twist it, and slam whoever it was to the bar would hit him immediately. But this place was all about touching.

Besides, Prophet knew that touch. "S'up Tom?"

Tom moved beside him, eyes narrowed. "What're you doing?"

"You said to come for a drink." Prophet held up another shot. "'S'what I'm doing. With Ray."

With Ray?

Only Prophet could manage to get pissed the way Tom wanted him to be and then quickly turn it around, accept the situation, and make it his. Which pissed Tom off. Again. Classic Prophet move. Tom tried to shake the pissed off-edness and went with command instead. "Come with me."

Prophet gave him the side-eye. His gaze held a little drunken amusement—and something else Tom had yet to place.

But he would.

"He's yours?" Ray, the big man in leather who was sitting way too close to Prophet for Tom's comfort looked between them.

There were so many ways Tom could answer that, several of them that could spike Prophet right through the heart. But the one that came out without hesitation was, "Better believe he's mine."

Ray stood. "Don't get fucking mouthy. He sat with me."

"I'll deal with him," Tom promised.

Prophet's brows raised. He looked between Tom and Ray. Ray shrugged and nodded at Tom, like he was planning on simply walking away from this. And no, that wouldn't fly at all, so he asked Ray, "You're not going to fight for me?"

"You want me to?" Ray asked.

"I think you should, yes," Prophet told him seriously.

And with that, Tommy actually goddamn rumbled, a volcano ready to fucking blow.

Prophet didn't care. He was out of control and just wanted to roll with it.

"Try it." Tom pushed Prophet—pushed him out of the way to go toe to toe with Ray. "See what you get."

"Or we could teach him a lesson," Ray offered.

"Okay, hold the phone." Prophet stared between Ray and Tom, because that wasn't how this was supposed to go. At all.

And how was *it supposed to go?*

He told himself to shut the fuck up, because he never planned shit like this. Knowing outcomes took the fun out of things, mainly because it raised the stakes. Upped the risks.

"I like the idea," Tom was saying.

"I most certainly don't," Prophet informed them and scanned the bar for another guy to flirt with who wouldn't turn on him.

Tom ignored Prophet in favor of asking Ray, "What do you have in mind?"

"I can get pretty creative. Boys like this usually need it." Ray looked at Prophet like he was some kind of prey.

"I'm no one's boy," Prophet muttered irritably.

Ray smiled. Like he thought Prophet was lying. "Bring him to the back," he told Tom before he walked in that direction.

"I'm not going to the back," Prophet called after him. Tom motioned to the bartender for another shot, which he promptly handed to Prophet.

"Drink."

"You're not drunk at all, are you?"

"Nope."

Prophet downed the shot and let Tom tug him through the crowded club and into one of the back rooms, where Ray waited. He pointed to the lone chair in the room, and Tom pushed Prophet toward it.

Prophet walked to it as slowly as he could. He could do the act of the petulant child better than anyone when he wanted to. And right now? He wanted to. But he did finally lower himself into the seat.

Ray stood next to the chair while Tommy came over and took Prophet's shirt off, tossing it aside. Tommy took Prophet's left nipple in between his thumb and forefinger and squeezed, then flicked the tip with his nail, making Prophet jump.

"Told you that if you were mine, I'd make you pierce it," Tom murmured as Ray started taking out equipment that looked like . . . piercing equipment.

"This." Prophet pointed a stabbing finger at each of them. Twice. "This was a setup."

"And you fell for it," Tom said calmly.

"I thought you were drunk."

"*You* definitely are," Tom observed.

"And you weren't hitting on me?" Prophet asked Ray.

"Technically no, but that doesn't mean I don't think you're cute." Ray smirked, and then gave him a once-over.

"Cute? Cute?" Prophet's voice rose until Tom pinched his nipple—again—to get his attention.

Prophet stared up at Tommy, in a little bit of a drunken haze, but mostly majorly turned on. Out of the corner of his eye, he noted Ray leaving the room.

He must've looked relieved, because Tom assured him, "Ray staying was never part of the plan."

"With Mal, it's not like this. I mean, shit . . . It's different. I stay in the room with Mal and whoever his dom is, because Mal doesn't have all that much trust." Prophet glanced at the piercing equipment and decided that it was time to distract. "But I did pick up some tricks."

"Yeah?" Tom looked like he was almost afraid to breathe, then asked, "Is it hard for you to watch?" Prophet frowned and tried to hide a smile until Tom pushed. "Come on—you know what I mean."

"Sometimes. I mean, I get it, the pain stuff. But it's not my thing. And he likes it rough."

"Needs it," Tom corrected.

"Needs it," Prophet conceded. "Do I give you what you need?"

Tom smiled easily. "Yeah, Proph. Always. And usually before I know I need it." He paused. "So Mal and I really aren't all that much different."

"Yeah, you are. Completely fucking different in many ways. Mal loves . . . needs pain."

"What kind of pain?" Tom asked, the interest apparent in his eyes.

Prophet shook his head. "The kinds you have to give me credit for knowing you won't like."

Tom nodded. Waited. A little tensely, and hell, they all had way too much tension these days. Prophet was actually surprised Mal hadn't called in one of these favors more frequently.

Finally, Tom said, "I'd only do it with you. I wouldn't want anyone else."

"Yeah, like I'd fucking let that happen," Prophet growled.

"I know, Proph." Tom smiled, then turned toward the equipment. He picked up an alcohol pad, but before he swiped it on Prophet's nipple, he bent, sucked the nipple hard into his mouth, making Prophet give a keening cry. He abused the fucking thing, twisted it until it was hard and angry, and then he wiped it down and reached for forceps.

It was only when he pulled Prophet's nipple out taut that he said, "I trained to do this."

Prophet looked up at him. "I trust you, Tommy."

Tom smiled. Then he picked up the needle and pushed it fast through Prophet's nipple, and holy mother of fuck, the line between pain and pleasure completely blurred as he saw the long, thin metal pole impaling his nipple.

Tom threaded the ring onto the needle and pulled it through the hole, which caused a whole other set of motherfucking pain that made him curse. Loudly. Tom glanced up at him, looking like he was holding back a laugh—the asshole—and then he released the forceps and set about closing the ring, which seemed like it took forever.

Prophet finally breathed when the forceps came off—how long he'd been holding it, he had no idea, but fuck, everything was reduced to the feeling of the piercing, the burning throb in his nipple, and that made it hard to focus on anything else. A long moment later, the ring was locked firmly in place, and Tommy was sinking to his knees in front of him, unzipping his pants and taking his hard cock down his throat.

Prophet shot immediately—and Tom had to know that would happen. Prophet knew he'd no doubt have come as he was being pierced . . . if he'd had Tom sucking him while Ray did the piercing. But that was interesting as a fantasy only.

Because this wasn't about sharing. Or payback. This was Tom showing him that he understood. That, no matter what, no matter how pissed they got, how much they fucked up . . . Prophet was his. Which was Tom's way of assuring that he wasn't going anywhere.

The music from outside the room suddenly pounded against the walls like it wanted in. It wasn't late, but this was the time for the club to get crowded.

Tom licked the crown of Prophet's cock as Prophet tried to catch his breath. "Lesson learned?"

"Definitely not," Prophet half scoffed, half panted.

Tom leaned in to suck Prophet again—a tease more than anything, but enough to make Prophet moan and shift. Then Tom looked up at him. "Because if you say yes, there's a chance I won't do something like this again, and you don't want that?"

Prophet didn't answer. Not with words. Instead, he pointed at him . . . but his other hand rubbed lightly over his newly pierced nipple.

And Tom had the only answer he ever needed.

He shook his head. "You can keep doing the favors for Mal."

Prophet glanced down at him. "Don't you think Cillian should be the one doing that now?"

Tom narrowed his eyes.

"I mean, since they're still hate-fucking sometimes," Prophet continued with an eye roll. "Do you think I don't notice things? Do all of you think I'm already blind?"

"Ah look, another blind joke. That's going well for you."

Prophet snorted. "You act like I'm not funny at all."

"You're a fucking laugh a minute."

"I'm not an idiot, Tommy."

No, and that made it harder to hide things from him. Tommy had figured they'd succeeded, but hell, Prophet might've seen through all of them from the start. "It's not my story."

"Could it have affected the mission?"

"Potentially. But we both know Mal wouldn't have allowed that," Tom reasoned.

"And Mal's in a good enough state of mind to make that judgment call himself, yes?" Prophet's voice held only the slightest twinge of sarcasm.

"None of us are in any kind of state of mind to make those kinds of judgment calls."

"That's why we run checks on each other," Prophet told him calmly and pointedly.

Fuck. It really sucked when Prophet was a hundred percent right and calm about it, because it took all the vigor out of Tom's fight. It was much easier when Prophet was being an ass. "I would never let anything compromise you or this mission."

Prophet acknowledged that with a nod. "I trust you, Tommy."

Tom sat back on his heels and pointed at Prophet's chest. Then smiled, even as he said, "Good. And don't plan on taking that out."

Prophet looked down at the ring through his nipple and pretended to scowl . . . even as Tom saw the smile breaking through. "Till when?"

"Till never. Punishment for cheating at Truth or Dare."

Yeah, Prophet would definitely be making that mistake again. Sometimes, it was too damned easy.

CHAPTER FOUR

P rophet was still half buzzed, although he was waning when they got back to the apartment . . . but Tommy was *quiet*. At first, Prophet thought he might be tired, which would be understandable . . . but it was more than that.

Tommy was restless.

He put his hand on Tommy's knee, which had been bouncing a hundred miles an hour as he sat on the couch, like he was waiting for . . . something.

"Sorry," Tommy said sheepishly. "That wound me up more than I realized."

Prophet slid a hand through his own hair, his nipple throbbing, reminding him of what had happened. Tommy had wanted to claim him—and he had. Maybe now it was Tommy's turn to be claimed. "That's not a bad thing—or unexpected, so don't worry about it."

"Thanks for letting me know how to feel," Tom muttered.

God, Tom felt like he was going insane and had no idea why.

Prophet gave him a small smile, and in turn Tom just muttered, "I need to shower."

He walked away, and Prophet didn't follow. Tom was both relieved and disappointed. And he had no idea why the hell he was jumping out of his skin right now. Even his teeth were set on edge, so he unclenched them, rubbing the sides of his jawline.

It'd been a great night. Worked out perfectly. Prophet'd loved it.

"So what the fuck's my problem?" he asked himself under the spray.

His cock gave him the answer. Prophet had been talkative—even teasing at the club—but Tom had seen the tiredness in his eyes. So he'd brought Prophet home, and Prophet had dozed on the couch while Tom made some dinner.

Now, it was midnight, and Tom needed to come. And yeah, that should solve everything. Even if it didn't, it'd feel good, so who cared?

He palmed his cock and rubbed along the piercings first, pulling them just enough to make him throb. He hissed at the pain and then fought a groan as he imagined Prophet doing this to him . . .

The glass door opened, the steam rushed out, and Prophet stood there, watching. Before Tom could say anything, Prophet ordered, "Don't stop now—jerk yourself, since you can't keep your hands off it."

"Since when do you fucking tell me what to do?" Tom demanded crankily. Of course, he kept on sliding his hand up and down his cock, partly because fuck, it was good—better when ordered, sure—and partly because the look in Prophet's eyes as he watched Tom doing it was just . . .

Fuck.

Fuck *yes*.

"Don't come though," Prophet told him casually, and look who had a second wind.

"Until when?" Tom gritted his teeth and slowed himself down.

"Until I say. Clear enough?"

Tom glared at him. Then, since glares never worked on Prophet anyway, he leaned his head back under the spray, letting water course over his body as he continued to work himself slowly.

A jolt make his gasp—and he opened his eyes to see Prophet flicking his nipple piercings casually. Twisting them. Smirking.

Fucker. Fucking motherfucking fucker.

Prophet was laughing. Maybe Tom'd said that out loud. He didn't know anything anymore, couldn't think, and that was exactly what Prophet was promising. He'd been on the receiving end of Prophet's orders enough times to know at least that.

He wasn't about to refuse. Not tonight and, he was pretty damned sure, not ever.

"Out of the shower, T. Right now." Prophet's voice was sharp enough to make Tom jump, mainly because he'd been buried in his own head. When he glanced at Prophet, he was pointing.

Tom smirked, because it would only make Prophet go harder on him. "Are you seriously ordering me around?"

"Are you seriously not going to fucking let me?" Prophet's words were a growl that went straight to Tom's dick.

"Point taken."

Prophet's eyes flashed. "Bed. Now."

Tom's gut tightened in anticipation. His nerve endings tingled, almost to the point of pain. There was nothing better than Prophet's undivided attention.

There was also nothing worse than that, but especially during sex . . . It was the pain-pleasure point most of the time.

Prophet was waiting with a towel outside the shower. Tom turned the water off and Prophet moved forward, patting him dry almost gently. Ignoring his cock, though, so too fucking gentle for Tom's tastes.

Prophet snorted, like he knew what Tom was thinking . . . not that hard to know, since he was rock hard. And then Prophet let the towel drop and pointed toward the bed. "Face down."

Tom sighed like he was being totally put out and tried not to run to the bed. He noted the ropes on the nightstand, and he swallowed hard as he stared at them, probably for a beat too long, before he lay down.

Tom was strong—could probably break the bed if he really had to get away—but he couldn't get out of Prophet's knots. He'd tried. And he'd tried to learn them well enough to be able to tie Prophet up . . . but so far, Prophet had always escaped.

Prophet loved that, of course.

Now, Prophet stroked Tom's hair. Tom had put his cheek down on the bed—Prophet had taken the pillows off the bed already—and he was facing away from Prophet. Prophet didn't ask him to turn to him, so Tom didn't. Instead, he just listened to Prophet.

"You asked me earlier about the pain," Prophet started, his voice husky, the way it always got when he was about to fuck Tom. "You also asked about you and Mal being the same, and I wasn't kidding. I know you like rough, but for you, it's not about the pain as much as it's about finally finding someone who can hold you down, hold you back . . . keep you in place when you lose it. But it's also got to be someone you trust. Not a stranger."

Tom shuddered at Prophet's words. No, he'd definitely never let a stranger do this to him. He couldn't think of anyone he would let besides the man doing so now, and decided that there was no use thinking about it. Wasn't going to happen.

Prophet had tied him down before—most notably in Etienne's studio in the bayou, and that had been when Tom had nearly lost it. Being tied had calmed him the fuck down. Prophet had worked on keeping him riled up and the sensations, the push-pull of both, had made the whole thing hotter.

"Look at me, Tommy," Prophet told him, and Tom did, lifted his head and put it down again so he was staring up at him. "Does that make sense to you?"

"Think you better show me . . . just so I can be sure," Tom urged, loving the slow smile that rolled across Prophet's face, finally reaching his eyes. Today, they held more blue than gray, thanks to the blue henley he wore, stretched across his chest. It looked good on him. Everything did.

Tom preferred him naked, though. But at least he could see the outline of Prophet's new piercing through the shirt. He reached out and just touched it lightly. Prophet drew in a quick breath—because yeah, still sore as shit—and smiled.

And yeah, he'd let Prophet do anything that he wanted to him.

The ropes were probably a bigger mind-fuck than anything else Prophet could do to Tommy right now—and they both knew it. Prophet white-knuckled through being tied down—for him, the pleasant torture came from forcing himself to remain still while unbound. But Tommy . . . Tommy needed that sensation, that weight, that presence that let him know that something—someone—stronger than he was at the moment was taking over. Taking it all away. And hell, Prophet could do that for him easily. Wanted to.

Because of that, Prophet took his time, making sure everything was looped and tied perfectly, until Tom was bound and spread to the head and footboards, with some rope tucked around his chest just for good measure. He'd forced Tom to push himself up as best as he could so Prophet could thread the ropes under him—and there was no real rhyme or reason for the way he was tied. The goal was to render Tom immobile and he was, although there was just enough give in the ropes so he could pull Tom onto his knees.

Barely though.

The sight of Tommy tied down to the bed, blindfolded . . . hell, that was now effectively burned into his brain. His dick got harder, which he hadn't thought possible, and a low growl escaped his throat. Or maybe it wasn't so low, because Tommy shuddered at the sound. Moaned.

And fuck, as much as Prophet loved hearing him, he also wanted to gag Tommy, watch him totally helpless. Mainly because it would turn Tommy the hell on.

But . . . baby steps. The blindfold was new—and hard enough. Harder on Prophet, because he was still learning to trust himself.

Prophet flexed his hands. Tommy would count on him when Prophet couldn't see well anymore. How would he be able to blindfold Tommy when he couldn't see well enough to check on him?

Then don't . . .

But then, Tom would spend more time worrying about Prophet, and Prophet wouldn't—couldn't—have that. So he'd have to learn, have to rely on his other senses to deal with this. Every situation would be different.

Deal with shit, one at a time, as it comes up.

The ropes holding him were soft, but the way they'd been tied gave Tommy just enough of that sting his body craved. Especially when he tugged to see how tight everything was, and then it burned, so he tugged again.

Prophet let him test the bonds for a long moment, before pulling his hips off the bed, forcing Tom to his knees. But his upper body was tied so well that he was unable to support himself on his arms. He was trapped, really and truly, with his chest exposed just enough for Prophet to slide a hand under him, pushing the mattress down.

Before Tom could wonder about that, his body jerked as Prophet put a clamp on his nipple—around the barbell—a fierce bite that took his breath away. He swallowed hard as a second one followed. Broad rough hands traced his bare back and he shuddered, more so when Prophet said, "We're just getting started, Tommy," then reached under and tweaked his nipple in the clamp.

"Fucker."

"Always a price for pleasure," Prophet said seriously. "But you already knew that."

Tom's arms were tied out to the sides a bit, making it harder for him to gain any purchase. And he definitely tried.

"Keep struggling," Prophet urged.

"Because it's useless?"

"Because it's fun to watch," he corrected.

Tom put his cheek down on the sheet. "Good. Then I surrender."

"I guess you don't need to come." But as he spoke, his tone was low and soothing, and he rubbed hard between Tom's shoulder blades. Hard enough to make Tom groan with pleasure.

"Just keep touching me."

Prophet did, one hand stroking, the other moving between Tom's legs. "Come on. Push up on your knees again."

Tom did, his shoulders and face pressed to the mattress, his ass spread and vulnerable.

He didn't bother to protest, not when Prophet was sliding a finger along his ass, brushing his hole. Then he inserted a lubed finger inside him, pressing hard.

Tom jolted. Was rewarded with a second finger and a third followed quickly. They twisted and stroked and pushed and he heard himself cursing. He'd ache in the morning from pulling so hard against the ropes, but he was good and bound . . . Prophet wasn't letting him go anywhere.

And for a second, just a second, that scared the fuck out of him, the way it was supposed to . . .

But he was safe. Didn't matter how bad the clamps burned. He could tell Prophet to stop all of it, and Prophet would. But the best part was that Tom would never have to do that. Prophet knew him too well . . . would always keep him safe, even as he pushed Tom's boundaries.

Prophet licked up the side of his neck. Tom shuddered again. "Killing me."

"And you love it." Prophet put his face down next to Tom's.

"Yeah, I do."

Prophet smiled, a sleepy, contented-as-fuck smile. "Me too, Tommy. Me too."

And finally, Prophet slid inside him, skin to skin—and that never got old. Tom tensed at the first burn—Prophet was careful but not easy—and goddamn, it would be so easy to just come. He bit the comforter hard enough to make his jaw ache in an effort to stop himself. Prophet slapped his ass twice—firm swats that made him want to come even more, the fucker.

And then Prophet took the clamps off simultaneously, and holy fuck, the rush of blood back to the nipples was a feeling so fused with his pain craving that it hit every single nerve in his body, like they were all ricocheting off his abused nipples. The pain forced Tom to move, and the only thing he could do semieffectively to get a feeling somewhere else besides the giant ache in his nipples was to rut back against Prophet until he heard the bed creak threateningly.

"If we break this bed . . ."

"I'll buy you a new one," Tom managed, because he was already seeing stars. "I just need you. Lije . . ."

At that, Prophet came in hard, hot spurts, his body shuddering, his fingers digging into Tom hard enough to bruise. "Now, Tommy . . ."

Tom didn't have to hear it twice, came with a fierce orgasm that he knew would knock him out in seconds, his entire body one giant throb.

It was surrender, complete and utter.

It was everything.

When he finally floated back to earth, Prophet was there, concern on his face . . . but also a look of contentment.

All Tom could do was tighten his grip on Prophet's hand—their fingers were already threaded together anyway and Tom was untied. He was still so floaty that he didn't register the pain from where the ropes had burned him—his own fault for pulling against them—but he could see the marks. And he loved them.

Prophet would worry about them, of course. And it was only then Tom realized that Prophet was looking at him in that way he had when his eyes had become blurry. Usually it was coupled with a barely veiled—if veiled at all—panic.

Now, there was none of that. Just Prophet, sitting there, holding his hands and watching Tom through the blur and shadow.

"You really liked that," Prophet asked after a long moment.

"Fuck, yeah." Tom's voice was raw and hoarse. Prophet reached around to the night table without looking and handed him a cup of water. Without spilling.

Tom didn't ask about his eyes, took and downed the water and then handed the cup back. "Intense. Couldn't do that a lot."

"That's another difference you and Mal have," Prophet told him, even as he reached into the nightstand drawer and pulled out moisturizer. He leaned forward, feeling for Tom's wrists, and began to rub the lotion into the sore parts, which made Tom smile and tear up at the same time. "Mal doesn't do it a lot, but he could."

"I can see that. Be good if he could find someone to do that all the time. The same person." Tom thoughts immediately went to Cillian. Tom had no clue if the guy was kinky or not, but he definitely didn't want to think too hard about it. Guess Cillian didn't mind public sex.

But all Prophet said was, "Everyone meets their match eventually."

Tom knew their hunger wasn't something that would level off. No, it was the opposite—it kept rising, twisting, feeding on itself . . . burning stronger, hotter. It wasn't going to change, partly because of their unpredictability.

They were quick to anger. Quicker to forgive.

There was so much they still had to go through. Times like this would be few and far between for the next months. But eventually . . . they'd have this again. Hotter than ever. "That's what I am—your match?"

Prophet smiled. Blinked a little, then looked serious. "You don't know that?"

Tom managed to move closer to Prophet, touched his newly pierced nipple, and whispered in his ear. "I like to hear you say it. That's all I need."

Read the *Hell or High Water* series
from the beginning.

Catch a Ghost
ISBN: 978-1-62649-039-0

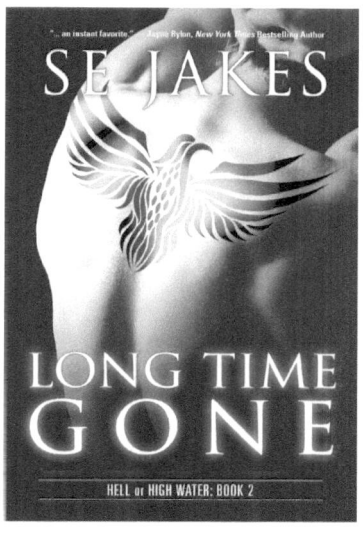

Long Time Gone
ISBN: 978-1-62649-061-1

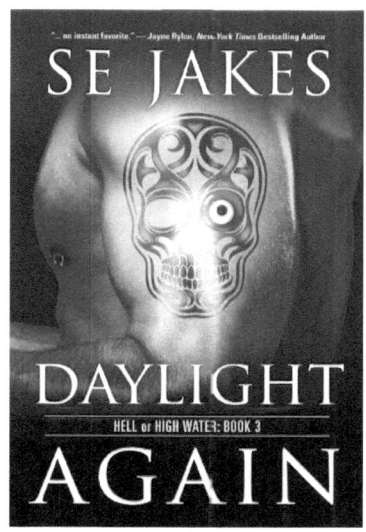

Daylight Again
ISBN: 978-1-62649-141-0

Dear Reader,

Thank you for reading SE Jakes's *Daylight Again*!

We know your time is precious and you have many, many entertainment options, so it means a lot that you've chosen to spend your time reading. We really hope you enjoyed it.

We'd be honored if you'd consider posting a review—good or bad—on sites like **Amazon, Barnes & Noble, Kobo, Goodreads, Twitter, Facebook, Tumblr,** and your blog or website. We'd also be honored if you told your friends and family about this book. Word of mouth is a book's lifeblood!

For more information on upcoming releases, author interviews, blog tours, contests, giveaways, and more, please sign up for our weekly, spam-free newsletter and visit us around the web:

Newsletter: tinyurl.com/RiptideSignup
Twitter: twitter.com/RiptideBooks
Facebook: facebook.com/RiptidePublishing
Goodreads: tinyurl.com/RiptideOnGoodreads
Tumblr: riptidepublishing.tumblr.com

Thank you so much for Reading the Rainbow!

RiptidePublishing.com

ACKNOWLEDGMENTS

Thanks to the usual suspects—my amazing (and patient) editor, Sarah Frantz, my publisher, Rachel Haimowitz, Alex Whitehall who always saves me with copy edits and proofs, and L.C. Chase, whose covers, we can all agree, are completely and utterly gorgeous. And to Riptide as a whole, because they are generally awesome.

To my group mods—Shawnie, Andrea, Susan C., and Lisa T—I couldn't do it without you guys. To my readers, because I hands down have the best ones out there. A special shout out to all of you guys who hang out at SE's Dirty Deeds, the Goodreads group, Twitter, and Tumblr.

As always, to my family, because they let me go into my fictional world and are always waiting with hugs—and meals—when I return. I love you.

ALSO BY SE JAKES

Havoc Motorcycle Club
Running Wild
Running Blind (2015)
Running on Empty (2016)

Hell or High Water (EE, Ltd.) Series
Catch a Ghost
Long Time Gone
Daylight Again
If I Ever (October 2014)

Men of Honor Series
Bound by Honor
Bound by Law
Ties That Bind
Bound by Danger
Bound for Keeps (EE, Ltd.)
Bound to Break

Standalone
Free Falling (EE, Ltd.)

Dirty Deeds (EE, Ltd.) Series
Dirty Deeds
Dirty Lies (coming soon)
Dirty Love (coming soon)

ABOUT THE AUTHOR

SE Jakes writes m/m romance. She believes in happy endings and fighting for what you want in both fiction and real life. She lives in New York with her family and most days, she can be found happily writing (in bed). No really . . .

SE Jakes is the pen name of *New York Times* best-selling author Stephanie Tyler (and half of Sydney Croft).

You can contact her the following ways:
Email: authorsejakes@gmail.com
Website: sejakes.com
Tumblr: sejakes.tumblr.com
Facebook: Facebook.com/SEJakes
Twitter: Twitter.com/authorsejakes
Instagram: instagram.com/authorsejakes
Goodreads Group: Ask SE Jakes

Truth be told, the best way to contact her is by email or in blog comments. She spends most of her time writing but she loves to hear from readers!